# Betsey Biggalow Is Here!

Also by Malorie Blackman

# Betsey Biggalow Is Here!

## Malorie Blackman

Illustrated by Jamie Smith

RED FOX

BETSEY BIGGALOW IS HERE!
A RED FOX BOOK 978 1 782 95185 8

First published in Great Britain in 1992 by Piccadilly Press Ltd

This edition published by Red Fox, an imprint of
Random House Children's Publishers UK
A Random House Group Company

This Red Fox edition published 2014

7 9 10 8 6

Text copyright © Oneta Malorie Blackman, 1992
Illustrations copyright © Jamie Smith, 2014

**Penguin Random House is committed to a sustainable future for
our business, our readers and our planet. This book is made from
Forest Stewardship Council® certified paper.**

MIX
Paper from
responsible sources

Addresses for companies within The Random House Group Limited can be found at:

THE RANDOM HOUSE GROUP Limited Reg. No. 954009

A CIP catalogue record for this book is available from the British Library.

Printed and bound in Great Britain by Clays Ltd, Elcograf S.p.A.

*For Neil and Lizzy,*
*with love as always.*

**Malorie Blackman** has written over sixty books and is acknowledged as one of today's most imaginative and convincing writers for young readers. She has been awarded numerous prizes for her work, including the Red House Children's Book Award and the Fantastic Fiction Award. Malorie has also been shortlisted for the Carnegie Medal. In 2005 she was honoured with the Eleanor Farjeon Award in recognition of her contribution to children's books, and in 2008 she received an OBE for her services to children's literature. She has been described by *The Times* as 'a national treasure'. Malorie Blackman is the Children's Laureate 2013–15.

# Contents

# The Special, Special Trainers!

Betsey peered in through the shoe shop window. There they were! Her special trainers. Her magic trainers. With those trainers she wouldn't just run, she'd *fly*! No one would be able to catch her in those extra special, *special* trainers.

"Betsey, come away from that window." Gran'ma Liz frowned.

"Oh, Gran'ma Liz. Look! The trainers I was telling you about — they're still there!" Betsey pointed.

"They're going to stay there too!" Gran'ma Liz said. "Come on."

"But I need a new pair of trainers," said Betsey. "Mine are worn to nothing now."

"I don't know how you can get through the soles of your shoes so fast." Gran'ma Liz tutted. "You must be eating them!"

"Gran'ma Liz, just look at these trainers. Look at the colours. Look at the laces. Look at the ..."

"Look at the time!" Gran'ma Liz glanced down at her watch. "Come on, Betsey, or we'll miss our bus."

"But Gran'ma Liz ..."

"Betsey, for the last time, I'm not buying

you those trainers. For weeks now, all your mum and I have heard from you is trainers this and trainers that!"

"But Gran'ma Liz, my best friend May has a pair of those trainers," Betsey said eagerly, "and you should see her when she runs. She doesn't run, she soars and swoops – just like a bird or a plane."

"Betsey, you talk some real nonsense sometimes," said Gran'ma Liz. "Come on, child."

So Betsey had to leave the front of the shoe shop. She crossed her fingers tight, tight, tight.

"I want those trainers something fierce," Betsey muttered to herself.

"What did you say, Betsey?" asked Gran'ma Liz.

"Nothing, Gran'ma," said Betsey.

"Hhmm!" said Gran'ma. And without another word, off they went home.

But on the way home, Betsey had an idea . . .

At dinner time, the family sat around the table — there was Gran'ma Liz, Mum, Betsey's bigger sister, Sherena, and Betsey's bigger brother, Desmond. For dinner there was cou-cou and flying fish and salad and a huge jug of delicious mango punch with plenty of ice. Betsey licked her lips. Scrumptious!

"Pass the salt please, Betsey," said Sherena.

Betsey picked up the glass salt shaker. "The tops of the trainers I want are just as

white as this salt," said Betsey.

She pointed to the pepper bottle.

"And the soles of the trainers I want are blacker than the writing on the pepper bottle." Sherena and Desmond looked at each other.

"Betsey, I don't want to hear any-more about those trainers. D'you hear?" Gran'ma Liz frowned.

"Yes, Gran'ma," Betsey said.

Betsey poured herself a glass of mango punch, but some spilt onto the sky-blue tablecloth. The yellow-orange liquid spread out.

"Betsey!" said Gran'ma Liz. "Look at that mess."

"That stain is just about the size of the trainers I want," Betsey murmured.

Gran'ma Liz could stand it no longer.

"Elizabeth Ruby Biggalow, all day, all week, all *month*, you've done nothing but mope and whine about those trainers." Gran'ma Liz frowned. "Your long face is spoiling my day as well as my dinner. Now not another word."

And Betsey knew then that she'd better shut up. Whenever Gran'ma Liz called her by her whole, full name, Betsey knew she was treading dangerously close to trouble.

But for the rest of the evening, all Betsey had in her head were her special trainers. She even fell asleep dreaming of soaring and flying, her special trainers on her feet.

The next morning, when Betsey went down for breakfast, everyone was unusually quiet.

"What's the matter?" asked Betsey.

"I've got something for you." Mum smiled. "As your old trainers are in such a state, I decided to get you some new ones."

"You bought the trainers!" Betsey couldn't believe it.

"Now perhaps we can all get some

peace," Gran'ma Liz sniffed.

Betsey grinned and grinned. Her extra special trainers. She'd got them at last. Mum handed over the bag she was hiding behind her back. Betsey opened the bag and . . .

"What's the matter?" asked Sherena.

"Oh!" Betsey couldn't say anything else. Her eyes started stinging and there was a huge, choking lump in her throat. Botheration! These weren't the trainers she wanted. Where were the ones with the white fronts and the black soles and the red laces? Where were her special trainers? Still in the shop – that's where!

These ones were pink and grey and didn't have any black writing on them like the ones she wanted.

"Betsey . . ." Gran'ma warned. "Your mum had to take time off work to buy those for you."

"Don't you like them, Betsey?" Mum asked.

"They're lovely," Betsey whispered.

"Put them on then," urged Desmond.

Betsey sat down and, oh so slowly, she put on her new shoes.

"They look boss!" Sherena smiled.

"The best trainers I've ever seen," said Desmond.

Gran'ma Liz didn't say anything. She just watched Betsey.

"Can I go and show them to my friend May, please?" Betsey asked Mum.

"Go ahead then." Mum smiled. "But don't stay with her too long. You've still got your morning chores to finish."

Betsey ran out of the kitchen. She couldn't wait to get out of the house. She looked down at her feet. These shoes weren't her special trainers. These shoes were just horrible. Betsey ran all the way to May's house – sprinting as if to run the trainers right off her feet. At May's house, Betsey knocked and knocked again. May opened the door. Worse still, May opened the door wearing the very same trainers that Betsey had wanted so much.

"Hi May," Betsey said glumly.

"Hi Betsey," said May. "I was just going to the beach. Coming?"

Betsey shrugged. "Just for a little while."

So off they went. But things weren't

right. No, they weren't. By the time Betsey and May reached the beach, they were having a full blown, full grown argument.

"Well, my trainers are the best in the country," said May.

"My trainers are the best in the world," Betsey fumed.

"Talk sense! My trainers are the best in the universe," said May.

"I hate you and your trainers," Betsey shouted. "And I hate these ones I'm wearing and I hate *everything*."

"And I hate you and your smelly shoes too," May stormed.

Betsey and May stared and glared and scowled and growled at each other.

Then Betsey started to smile, then to laugh, then to hold her stomach she was laughing so much.

"What's so funny?" May asked, still annoyed.

"Botheration! Imagine hating a pair of shoes!" Betsey laughed. "You hate my shoes and I hate your shoes. And both pairs of shoes are probably laughing at us for being so foolish."

"All this fuss over a pair of trainers," May agreed with a giggle.

"Come on! Let's have a run. Things are always better after a run on the beach," said Betsey. "I'll race you to that palm tree yonder."

"Ready . . . steady . . . go!"

And off they both sprinted, faster than fast. They leapt over the sand and through the lapping water, kicking up the spray as they went, laughing and laughing. Until finally, they both collapsed in the shade of the palm tree Betsey had pointed to. Who won the race? Neither May nor Betsey cared.

Betsey glanced down at her wet shoes. They were all right! Not the ones she'd wanted, but a present from her mum just

the same. A special present. A wonderful surprise.

"Look at that!" said May, surprised. May pointed to her trainers. The red colour in her laces was running down the white front of her trainers and over the black writing. May's trainers didn't like getting wet − not one little bit. Betsey glanced down at her own trainers − still grey and pink and no running colours anywhere. She jumped up.

"May, let's walk along the beach for a bit longer," said Betsey. "We can collect shells and paddle. Never mind our trainers. Let's walk along in our bare feet."

"Yeah! It's much nicer walking on the sand in bare feet anyway," May agreed.

And May and Betsey ran over the white sand and through the blue water, their trainers knotted at the laces and dangling around their necks.

# Betsey Biggalow
# Is Here!

Betsey Biggalow had another of her bright and shiny ideas! Today would be her HELP THE WORLD day! The question was, who should she help first? She ran into the living room. Sherena was sitting at the table, books, books and more books spread out in front of her.

"Have no fear! Betsey Biggalow is here!" said Betsey proudly.

"Not now, Betsey. Can't you see I'm busy?" said Sherena.

Betsey walked across to peer over her sister's shoulder.

"What are you doing?"

Sherena looked up, annoyed. "I'm trying, *trying* to revise for my maths test on Monday."

"I'll help you," Betsey insisted.

"You can help me by disappearing," Sherena said crossly. "Go on! Vanish! Depart! Leave! Go away!"

"All right. You don't have to go on," said Betsey. "If you don't need my help, I'll go and find someone who does."

"You do that!" said Sherena, burying her head back in the book in front of her.

Betsey ran out into the backyard to see her brother. Desmond was feeding the chickens which clucked and pecked and pecked and clucked.

"Have no fear! Betsey Biggalow is here!" said Betsey. "I've come to help."

"I don't need the help of a shrimp like you," Desmond scoffed. "Besides, how

come you wait till I've almost finished,
before coming to help me?"

"Well, I'm here now," said Betsey.
Helping the world was turning out to be
more difficult than she'd ever imagined.

"Betsey Biggalow, what are you up to?"
Gran'ma Liz came out into the yard. "If
you're seeking useful employment, I can
soon find a hundred and one things for
you to do."

Betsey shuddered. She was looking for one interesting something to do – not a hundred and one boring things!

"No thanks, Gran'ma Liz," said Betsey. "I was just about to go and see my friend May."

"Hhmm!" said Gran'ma Liz. "Well, just make sure you're back before supper."

Betsey didn't need to be told twice. It was time to scarper before Gran'ma Liz decided that her one hundred and one things should come before a visit to May.

So off Betsey went, down the track, along the road, to May's house. The evening sun was still hot, hot, hot and the sugar cane in the fields on either side of the road cast long, evening shadows.

"Botheration! So much for 'Have no fear, Betsey Biggalow is here!'" Betsey muttered with disgust.

And so much for helping the world.

You just couldn't help the world when it didn't want your help! Betsey was so deep in thought that she almost didn't hear it. She stopped and frowned and looked around. Then it came again.

"Help . . . oh, please help me . . ."

Frightened, Betsey looked around. "Who's that? Who's there?"

"Over here . . ." the faint voice said.

Slowly, oh so slowly and oh so carefully, Betsey crept over towards the voice.

Then she saw him. There, lying in a ditch by the side of the road, was a man with a moustache. He was lying half on his side, half on his back. And there, on top of his left leg, was a motorbike.

"I . . . I think I've broken my leg," the man whispered. Betsey could see the perspiration all over his cheeks and his chin. His wet face glistened in the evening sunshine. His shirt was damp and sticking to him just as closely as Gran'ma Liz's Sunday hat stuck to her head.

"Wait . . . wait there. I'll go and get my gran'ma," Betsey said. "I'll be right back."

"What's your . . . your name . . ." asked the man.

"Betsey. Betsey Biggalow."

"Hurry, Betsey . . ." the man gasped, before his eyes closed and his head nodded down towards the ground.

Betsey ran. She raced like the wind.

"Gran'ma Liz! Gran'ma Liz! There's a man. And he's broken his leg. And he's lying in a ditch. And his motorbike is lying on his leg. And his eyes are closed. And . . ."

"Calm down, child." Gran'ma Liz frowned. "Now what're you saying?"

So Betsey explained all over again. The words fell over each other, each one in a rush to be heard. Desmond came in from the garden and Sherena left her books in the living room to listen. By the time Betsey had finished explaining she was out of breath.

"You'd better take us to him," Gran'ma Liz said. Gran'ma Liz got a blanket and off they all went. At last they reached the part of the road where Betsey had seen the man and his motorbike in the ditch. And he was still there, his eyes closed, his body as still as Sunday morning.

"Sherena, run back to the house and phone for an ambulance. Desmond, Betsey, help me move this motorbike off his leg." Gran'ma Liz got busy at once.

"Is he all right?" Desmond puffed as they tried to shift the motorbike.

"He's still breathing and that's something," said Gran'ma Liz. "He's unconscious. The pain was probably too much."

"Should we move him?" asked Betsey.

"No. When someone's been in a road accident you shouldn't move them. The paramedics will know the right way to move him," Gran'ma Liz said. "I'll cover him with this blanket I brought with me."

"Why does he need a blanket? It's hot-baking!" said Betsey.

"Anyone who's had a shock should be kept warm. You can get cold very quickly when you've had a serious accident. We'll stand and watch over him until the ambulance arrives."

"Look, Gran'ma Liz. The front tyre of his bike is flat." Desmond pointed. "He must have got a puncture and skidded off the road."

"If the good Lord had meant for us to go tearing around to up, down, below and above, we would have petrol in our bodies, not blood," Gran'ma Liz sniffed. Gran'ma Liz didn't approve of fast cars and faster motorbikes.

After what seemed like ages an ambulance finally arrived, its lights flashing, its siren wailing. Betsey watched, holding her breath, as the paramedics lifted the man with the broken leg onto a stretcher. The injured man's eyes fluttered open and saw Betsey.

"It's OK. You're going to the hospital now," said Betsey.

"Thank you, Betsey." The man smiled. "I'm going to be fine now." And he closed his eyes as he was carried over to the

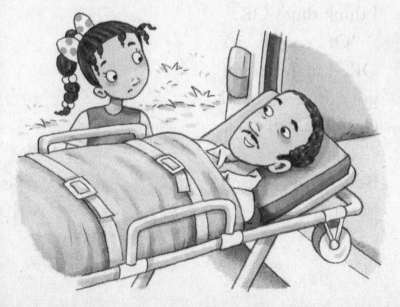

ambulance. In only a few moments, the ambulance went roaring away towards the hospital, its siren wailing.

"Will the man and his leg be all right?" asked Betsey.

"He'll be fine. At the hospital they'll fix him up in no time." Gran'ma Liz smiled. "Betsey, you did very well. You were right to come and get me."

Betsey thought hard for a moment.

"I didn't help the whole world today," she said. "But I did help a little bit of it. I think that's OK."

"Of course it's OK. I'm proud of you, Betsey," said Gran'ma Liz.

And what did Betsey do? Betsey just smiled.

# Betsey and the Mighty Marble

'I've got a marble. A mighty marble," said Josh proudly. School had finished for the day and there was still plenty of afternoon left to play in. Betsey and her friends were at the beach.

"Who wants to look at my mighty marble?" Josh called out.

"Me! Me!" everyone shouted.

Josh held out his marble in the palm of his hand. Betsey's brown eyes sparkled brighter than sunshine on the clear blue sea behind her. Ooooh! All eyes were on Josh's marble. Oh, how it glittered! Oh, how it glistened! Betsey had never seen anything like it.

"I told you," said Josh. "Isn't it terrific?"

It was the biggest marble Betsey had ever seen and it was filled with sky blue and leaf green and moonlight silver slivers.

"It's the most beautiful marble in the world," Betsey breathed. And all at once, she wanted that marble. She wanted that marble something fierce.

"Josh," began Betsey, holding up her bag of marbles. "I'll swap you ten of my best marbles for your mighty marble."

"No way," Josh scoffed. "Mr Mighty Marble is staying with me!"

"I'll swap you *twenty* of my marbles for your mighty marble," said May.

Soon the air was filled with 'I'll swap you this" and "I'll swap you that", but Josh only laughed and held Mr Mighty Marble up higher.

Betsey looked at the super marble in Josh's hands. It called out to her, teasing her.

"Betsey ..." whispered Mr Mighty Marble. "Betsey, look at me. Aren't I just the most perfect, the most splendid marble in the world?" And what could Betsey reply but, "You are! You are!"

Betsey dug her hand into her dress pocket and slowly took out Old Faithful.

Old Faithful was a small marble, perfect and clear, with a single gold streak like a summer lightning flash caught in its middle. Betsey's dad had given it to her.

"You look after Old Faithful," said Dad. "And Old Faithful will look after you."

It was Betsey's special marble and all her friends admired it, but Betsey never played with it. Old Faithful was too small to play with.

"Josh," said Betsey. "Let's have a contest, right now. Your Mr Mighty Marble against my best marble."

"Why should I?" Josh frowned.

"Because if you win, I'll give you every marble I've got," said Betsey slowly. She held up her full bag of marbles. "You'll get every single marble in here."

Josh's eyes gleamed. "Including Old Faithful?"

Betsey looked at
the marble her dad
had given her. Next to
Mr Mighty Marble, Old
Faithful looked dull and titchy-tiny
and hardly worth bothering with at all.

"Including Old Faithful," Betsey agreed
at last.

"Betsey! You can't do that," said May.
"Your dad gave you Old Faithful."

"May, don't you worry," said Betsey.
"If I win, I'll get Josh's super marble."

"And what happens if you lose?" asked
May, her hands on her hips.

Betsey thought about it, long and hard.
If she lost then Josh would end up with
every single marble she had in the world
– including Old Faithful. Dad had played
marbles with Old Faithful when he was
a boy and he'd given her Old Faithful as
a present. How could she give away a

present from her dad? She shouldn't have told Josh she'd give him Old Faithful. What if she *did* lose and Dad found out?

"Josh, I think . . ." Betsey began.

"You're not changing your mind, are you? You're not turning chicken?" Josh called out. "Cluck! Clu-uu-ck! Chicken!"

"No, I'm not. I'm ready when you are," said Betsey. But as she spoke she was careful not to look at May. That didn't mean that she couldn't hear May tutting beside her, though.

Josh walked to his starting position which was at the end of the path that led to the beach. Everyone followed him. May pulled Betsey back from the crowd.

"Betsey, you're making a big mistake." May shook her head.

"Botheration, May! You're not my gran'ma. Don't you try to boss my head," said Betsey, annoyed.

"Are you really going to let Josh take all your marbles?" asked May. "Even the one your dad gave you?"

"I'm going to win Josh's mighty marble," Betsey said stubbornly. "So Josh won't get any of my marbles. I won't lose a single one of them."

"You've lost your marbles already if you think your itsy-bitsy bit of glass stands a chance against Josh's mighty marble," said May.

Betsey began to feel bad. Worse than bad. Betsey began to feel terrible. She wished she'd never challenged Josh to this stupid contest.

"Come on then, Betsey," Josh called out. "I'm busting to win a whole bag of marbles."

Betsey and May walked over to join Josh and the others.

"Josh, we can still have our contest but I don't want to include Old Faithful in it. My dad gave me Old Faithful and . . ."

But Josh didn't let Betsey finish.

"Cluck! Clu-uu-ck! Chicken!" Josh began to leap about and to peck and flap and strut, just like a chicken. "Cluck! Clu-uu-ck!"

Soon everyone else was doing the same thing. "Clu-uu-ck!"

"Botheration!" said Betsey. "Josh, you're about to lose Mr Mighty Marble."

Betsey dug into her bag.

"What are you doing?" Josh frowned.

"Getting out a marble to play with," answered Betsey.

"You've got to use Old Faithful," Josh said. "That was the deal."

"But that's not fair. Your mighty marble is ginormous and Old Faithful is tiddly," said Betsey.

"Too bad. That's the deal." Josh smiled.

What could Betsey do? The contest was all her idea so she couldn't back out now. There was nothing left to do but to stay put and play. Betsey felt her eyes stinging but she forced herself not to cry. She was going to lose all her precious marbles. All the marbles it had taken her so long to collect. And worse still, she was going to lose Old Faithful.

"Josh, you go first," sniffed Betsey.

And the contest began. Everyone gathered round to watch. Josh flicked Mr Mighty Marble first. Betsey flicked Old Faithful away from Mr Mighty Marble. Josh flicked his marble towards Betsey's.

"Ooooh!" A gasp came from everyone

around. Josh had only just missed Betsey's marble.

This was it. If Betsey didn't do something, Josh would hit her marble with his very next shot and then Betsey would lose every single marble she had in the world.

"Bombsies!" Betsey said.

Josh laughed. "Bombsies! With that little marble! You can't win, Betsey, so give up now."

"I'll show you," Betsey said. She stood up, Old Faithful in her hand. She stood over Josh's marble, carefully lining up Old Faithful over Mr Mighty Marble. If she missed, Josh would win for sure. No one spoke. The only sound came from the waves lapping on the white sand and the sound of birds singing from the trees.

"Your hand can't be lower than your waist," Josh said.

"I know." Betsey didn't look up. She carried on lining up her shot until Old Faithful was directly above Mr Mighty Marble. Then Betsey let go of her own marble. Old Faithful hit Mr Mighty Marble with a CRR-AAA-CK!

Then a strange

thing happened. Old Faithful bounced off Mr Mighty Marble.

"Ooooh!" said everyone.

Josh's marble wasn't well. It wasn't well at all. Mr Mighty Marble, Mr Super Marble, Mr Bigger-than-anyone-else's Marble had cracked into four pieces. Each piece lay on the path, glistening and glittering just as loudly as before.

Betsey picked up Old Faithful and stared at it.

"Wow, Betsey. That's some marble," everyone said.

Josh carefully picked up the pieces that made up what used to be Mr Mighty Marble.

"Look what you did." Josh stared down at the pieces in his hand.

"Mr Mighty Marble doesn't look so mighty any more." May laughed.

"Sorry, Josh," Betsey said. "You can have any five of my marbles if you want." Betsey held out her bag of marbles.

"Can I have Old Faithful?" Josh asked hopefully.

"No chance!" said Betsey firmly. "Old Faithful may be small, but he's a real super marble."

Josh looked down and kicked at the ground with the toe of his right shoe.

"Come on, Josh." Betsey smiled. "I'll give you my second best marble instead."

"Oh, all right then," Josh said at last. Betsey handed over her bag and let Josh pick out five marbles he wanted.

Then Betsey, May and all their friends set off for home, telling tales of Old Faithful, the mightiest marble of them all.

# Betsey's Bad Day!

The moment Betsey opened her eyes, she was awake. She grinned and sat up. Saturday morning! And only one more week until Dad came home. And no school! *And* they were all going into town today. Today was going to be a good day!

"Yippee! Saturday!" Betsey sprang out of bed.

She put on her slippers and went to have her shower. When she'd finished, she went for her breakfast. Sherena and Desmond were already at the table. So was Gran'ma Liz.

"Sit down, Betsey," said Mum. "I'll get your breakfast." Betsey turned in her chair to look at Mum.

"What's for breakfast, Mum?" Betsey sniffed the air. "Ham?"

"And scrambled eggs," said Mum.

"Scrumptious." Betsey grinned. She turned around. There before her was a long, cool glass of orange juice.

"Yumptious-scrumptious!" said Betsey. And she picked up the glass and started to drink. Ooh, it was cold! Ooh, it was refreshing! Ooh, it was delicious!

"Betsey, you toad! That's *my* orange juice," said Desmond.

"Then what's it doing in front of my plate?" Betsey replied.

"I don't know and I don't care," said Desmond. "It's still my orange juice."

"Desmond boy, don't call your sister a toad," said Gran'ma Liz. "If she's a toad,

then you must be one too because you're her brother." Desmond started to sulk.

"Desmond, there's plenty of orange juice for everyone, so behave," said Mum. "And Betsey, if you want some orange juice, pour some for yourself. Don't just help yourself to your brother's."

"But . . . but . . ." Betsey protested. Botheration! The glass *had* been in front of her plate. Never mind, today was

*Saturday*! Betsey handed over the now half empty glass to Desmond.

"Huh!" said Desmond, still sulking. He put the glass to his lips and finished his orange juice with one gulp. Then he poured himself another one.

"Pass the sugar, Betsey," said Sherena, stirring her coffee.

"Manners!" said Gran'ma Liz. "What do you say?"

"Please," said Sherena. "Please, please, please!"

With a grin, Betsey handed over the sugar bowl. Sherena added a spoonful of sugar to her coffee, then another spoonful, then another, and another.

"Sherena girl, by the time you're sixteen, you'll not have one tooth left in your head if you carry on like that," said Gran'ma Liz.

"I like it sweet, Gran'ma Liz." Sherena

smiled. "Besides, I want to put on weight. I'm as skinny as a needle – worse luck. Everyone says so." Sherena lifted her coffee cup to her lips. She'd barely taken one sip when immediately she started to gag and cough. The cup fell from her hand. Both hands flew to her throat, as she coughed and spluttered and coughed some more, her eyes watering.

"Sherena? Sherena, what's the matter?" Mum ran over to her and so did Gran'ma Liz. Betsey sprang out of her chair. "Sherena, are you all right?"

"Salt!" Sherena coughed. "There's s-salt in that bowl, not s-sugar."

"Whose turn was it to fill the sugar bowl last night?" Mum frowned. All eyes turned slowly to Betsey. Betsey's mouth dropped open.

"I thought I put sugar in it — honest!" she said quickly. Mum took the sugar bag and the salt bag out of the cupboard.

"Which bag did you use?" she asked.

Betsey stared at the bags. One was white and red, the other was red all over. The first bag said SALT on it and the second bag said FINEST SUGAR.

"Er . . . I . . . er . . ." began Betsey.

"I'm waiting, Betsey." Mum pursed her lips.

"I used the white and red bag to fill the sugar bowl," Betsey admitted, adding quickly, "But it wasn't my fault. The salt bag was on the kitchen table and I thought it was the sugar bag and I was in a hurry because I was missing a film on the T.V. . . ."

"More haste, less speed." Gran'ma Liz wagged her finger.

Mum frowned. "Betsey! What is the matter with you today? First you drink you brother's orange juice, then you try to poison your sister."

"But it wasn't purpose work," said

Betsey. "I didn't do it deliberately. I only ..."

"Betsey, if you carry on like this, we'll leave you with May's parents and go to town without you," said Mum. "If I take you into town, goodness only knows what havoc you'll cause."

"I won't cause any havoc, Mum. I promise," Betsey said quickly. She didn't want to miss the trip into town. No, she didn't!

"So you say," said Mum. "But you've only been awake for five minutes and look what's happened already."

Betsey couldn't argue with that so she said nothing. She thought a lot though. And her thoughts started with "botheration" and ended with "botheration"!

At least it's Saturday – and only seven

more days till Dad comes home, Betsey thought to herself. That thought cheered her up a little.

After breakfast, they all had to hurry up and get ready in order to catch the bus into town. In her bedroom, Betsey kicked off her slippers and looked around for the pink and grey trainers her Mum had bought her. She found one by the bedroom door where she and Sherena always left their shoes, but could she find the other one? No, she couldn't! Betsey searched high and low, under the bed and in the bottom of the wardrobe.

"Betsey! Speed up!" Mum called out.

"Coming, Mum," Betsey called back. Betsey hunted to the left of the bedroom and to the right of the bedroom and she still couldn't find her other trainer.

"BETSEY!" Mum said. "What are you doing? We're going to miss our bus."

"Mum, I can't find one of my trainers," Betsey yelled.

"Then wear your sandals, but hurry up! That bus won't wait for ever."

Betsey stood in the middle of the room, her hands on her hips. Botheration! Double botheration! Where *was* that other trainer?

"Betsey!" Mum came into the room. "Come on."

"But Mum, I wanted to wear my trainers," Betsey said.

Mum looked around the room. She pointed under the chest of drawers. "Isn't that your other shoe?"

Betsey looked down. There, just sticking out from the bottom of the chest of drawers was the other trainer.

"But Mum, I didn't put my trainer there . . ." Betsey said, puzzled.

"It didn't crawl under there by itself, Betsey. What has got into you this morning?" Mum sighed. "Now, put on your trainer and let's go."

At last they left the house. Desmond walked with Gran'ma Liz and Sherena walked with Mum. Betsey walked by herself behind everyone else. They were all talking and laughing. Everyone except Betsey.

"I might as well call today My-Bad-Day instead of Saturday," Betsey muttered to herself. "Seems like everything I touch is going wrong and nothing I do is going right."

Betsey sighed and sighed some more. Gran'ma Liz turned around.

"Betsey, we're off to town." Gran'ma Liz smiled. "So put your face straight before the wind changes direction and your face is stuck with that gloomy look on it. We'll get our shopping and when we've finished we can all go for an ice-cream."

Ice-cream! Scrumptious! Double Scrumptious! That was more like it!

The bus came along and juddered to a halt just as they all reached the bus stop.

"Jump up! Jump up!" laughed Gran'ma Liz. "We're off to town!"

And they all scrambled aboard. Soon they'd reached the market in town.

The town was even busier and better

than Betsey remembered. They didn't come to town too often as there were plenty of small shops locally. But about once a month, they all climbed aboard a bus and went shopping for the things they couldn't buy from the local shops. Betsey sniffed the air. She could smell plantain cooking and fried fish and all different kinds of fruit like freshly picked bananas and mangoes and paw-paws and coconuts. Yumptious-scrumptious!

Betsey grinned. Saturday felt better already. Then Betsey saw something that made her eyes open wide as plates and made her mouth drop open and made her heart beat faster than fast. There, across the street. Dad!

"Dad! DAD!" Betsey yelled out.

Dad heard Betsey's voice and turned. He grinned and waved and once the road was clear, ran across it. Dad! There followed such huggings and cuddlings.

"I wasn't expecting you for another week." Mum smiled happily.

"My last exam wasn't meant to be until the end of next week but they brought it forward so I've finished all my exams now." Dad grinned. "I decided not to tell you all but to surprise you. My plane landed about an hour ago."

"Are you a doctor yet?" Betsey asked eagerly.

"Not yet, Betsey." Dad shook his head. "I've got one more year of studying to do first."

"So how long are you going to be home for?" asked Gran'ma Liz.

"A few weeks." Dad grinned. "The

exams are over and I'm on holiday."

"Yippee!" Sherena and Desmond shouted.

"I knew it." Betsey smiled. "I knew today was going to be a good day!"

And she was right.

# Have you read these other
## Betsey Biggalow books?